It's five years since Ben Tennyson last transformed into aliens and fought crime with his cousin Gwen and their Grandpa Max.

Now 15 years old, Ben is once again forced to turn to the Omnitrix to help fight a new and more sinister threat – the HighBreed, DNAliens and the Forever Knights, who team up to take over the world.

The watch-like Omnitrix has re-programmed itself and has a complete set of ten, brand new alien choices for Ben to get to grips with. Helped by his cousin Gwen with her magical powers and Ben's former enemy, Kevin E. Levin, Ben is soon all set to go hero once again!

NOW READ ON . . .

EGMONT

We bring stories to life

This edition first published in Great Britain 2010
by Egmont UK Limited
239 Kensington High Street
London W8 6SA

Adapted by Barry Hutchison

1 3 5 7 9 10 8 6 4 2

Printed and bound in Great Britain

The Forest Stewardship Council (FSC) is an international,
non-governmental organisation dedicated to promoting
responsible management of the world's forests. FSC operates
a system of forest certification and product labelling that
allows consumers to identify wood and wood-based products
from well-managed forests.

For more information about Egmont's paper buying policy,
please visit www.egmont.co.uk/ethicalpublishing
For more information about the FSC, please visit their
website at www.fsc.org

ALONE
TOGETHER

CHAPTER ONE

GONE

Laser blasts erupted around Ben's head, blasting holes in the wall behind him. Ducking behind a stack of boxes, he spun the dial on the Omnitrix, keeping one eye on the HighBreed who had been shooting at him.

The towering alien turned and launched a bundle of deadly spikes towards Gwen, who was taking cover behind a pillar. She waited for them to clatter to the floor before risking a glance at the HighBreed.

'It's trying to run,' she yelled. 'Cut it off!'

Kevin launched himself from one of the warehouse's many shadows, landing heavily on the HighBreed's back. He fired a punch against the side of its head, but if the alien felt it he didn't show it. With a twitch of his shoulders he threw Kevin into a stack of wooden boxes.

'I've got it covered,' Ben cried, making straight for the HighBreed and slapping a hand down hard against the face of the Omnitrix. The Omnitrix projected a bright green light across the warehouse. In a flash Ben transformed into the alien form known as Echo Echo.

Still running, Echo Echo split into six identical clones of himself. Together they surrounded the HighBreed, cutting off his escape. 'Going somewhere? I don't think so!' they all said at once.

The HighBreed raised both fists above his head and then slammed them down against the stone floor. As the ground shook, the six Echo Echoes were thrown backwards, off balance.

Shrieking, Gwen hurled five energy balls at the HighBreed, one after another. They hit him hard, staggering him enough for Kevin to rush in and land a punch. In his stone form, Kevin was strong – really strong. The force of the punch lifted the HighBreed off his feet. The ground shook again as he landed on his back with a thump.

Kevin picked up one of the Echo Echoes and scowled at him. 'Nice going Mr "I've got it covered". Not much help there.'

'Hey, I'm all over it!' chimed the clones, sprinting past Kevin to where the HighBreed was getting to his feet. The clones swarmed all over the enormous alien, holding onto his arms and legs and wrapping their stubby arms tightly around his head.

'Don't touch me, creature,' spat the HighBreed, squirming as he tried to shake the little aliens off. As he struggled, his eyes fell on a large piece of machinery that was half-hidden in the corner of the warehouse. Slowly, he dragged himself towards it.

'Don't let him get in that thing,' barked Kevin. 'It's a teleporter pod.'

Bending, Kevin tore a chunk of concrete from the floor and hurled it towards the teleporter. It struck the side of the machine and an explosion of blue sparks fizzed from inside the control panel.

'You've damaged the transmission field, you stupid human!' roared the HighBreed. Still wrestling with the six Echo Echo clones, he tried to turn. A big flash of blue energy hit him like a lightning bolt. He felt his feet slip from under him.

The HighBreed's scream echoed around the warehouse as the blue light became blindingly bright. Gwen and Kevin shielded their eyes unable to look at the glow.

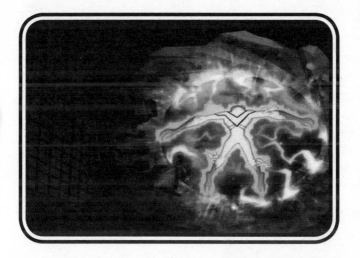

They opened their eyes just in time to see the HighBreed – with the Echo Echoes still holding onto him – being sucked into the teleporter. The machine shook violently for a moment, before becoming still. The blue glow faded to darkness.

'Ben!' cried Kevin.

But Ben was gone.

One by one the Echo Echo clones landed heavily on the sandy ground of a barren desert. The HighBreed alien loomed above them, his fists clenched.

'Microcephalic, vermin-ridden carcass,' he bellowed.

The Echo Echoes leapt to their feet. 'That's an insult, right?' they asked.

'Your friend interfered with the teleporter settings. He is a fool.'

'Well, to be fair, we were more than a little distracted,' replied Echo Echo. 'What with you trying to kill us and all.'

'That's right, I was,' nodded the HighBreed. 'In fact, I still am.'

He swung down at the closest clone with a punch that would surely have knocked its head clean off. But Echo Echo was fast.

He dodged left, out of harm's way, then opened his mouth and hit the HighBreed with a sonic scream.

The HighBreed skidded backwards across the sand, stunned but not hurt. He was about to attack again when he felt a tremor underneath him. Then the entire desert started to rumble.

Echo Echo frowned. 'Whoa. Um . . . was that an earthquake?'

The HighBreed was about to answer when he felt the ground move beneath his feet. He threw himself out of the way just as a giant, worm-like head erupted from the sand.

'This isn't good,' Echo Echo muttered.

The worm-creature pushed up and up, stretching from the ground until it stood as tall as a skyscraper. Echo Echo peered up at him.

'Whoa,' he cried, 'think I'm gonna need some back-up here!'

In a blur of green, Echo Echo split into a dozen more copies of himself. They all looked up in time to see the worm-creature diving towards them, its gaping mouth wide open.

'Now let's try this again!' they yelled, opening their own mouths almost as wide as the monster's. Working as one they blasted the worm with their sonic screams. The creature thrashed around for a few moments, then slammed its head against the sand and burrowed back below ground.

The desert fell deadly silent, but not for long. A few seconds later, the ground beneath

Echo Echo's feet began to tremble.

'Not good, not good!' the clones chimed.

KRRRRAAAAWK!

The worm-creature's head burst through the ground directly below one of the clones. It flashed its pointed teeth, then swallowed the Echo Echo whole!

The other clones watched on, horrified, unsure of what to do next. Suddenly, the worm-creature began to gag and choke. With a final splutter he coughed up the Echo Echo clone, sending him rocketing towards the others. The little alien collided with his fellow clones, knocking them down like skittles.

The worm-creature then turned and fixed his gaze on the HighBreed. The little creature had not tasted good. Perhaps the larger one would taste better!

'HighBreed, look out! Run!' cried Echo Echo, as the giant worm began to race after the fleeing HighBreed.

As he darted across the desert, the HighBreed turned and fired energy bolts up at his pursuer. The worm-creature didn't even slow down.

Merging back into a single being, Echo Echo hopped up on to the worm's tail and raced along its slimy back. When he was somewhere near the head, he took a deep breath and unleashed a sonic scream. This time he focused the full strength of the blast at where he guessed the monster's brain would be.

The worm shrieked loudly and began to thrash around in pain on the sand. Seizing his chance, the HighBreed fired one energy bolt after another, concentrating on the spot Echo Echo was attacking.

As the blasts struck the worm, it decided enough was enough. Echo Echo only just managed to leap from the monster's back, before it buried itself deep back into the sandy desert floor.

'What was that thing?' asked Echo Echo, when he was sure the creature had gone.

'A Dravek. Its kind is numerous on this deadly planet.'

Echo Echo nodded. 'Then we'd better get off this planet before any more of them show up. We don't want to bump into one of those in the night!'

The HighBreed scowled. 'We? What exactly do you mean by "we", filthy human?'

'Yes, dear HighBreed – "we",' replied Echo Echo. 'You couldn't defeat it alone, and I couldn't defeat it alone. If more of them come our only hope of survival is if we fight together!'

CHAPTER TWO

AN UNEASY ALLIANCE

From the HighBreed's body language Echo Echo could tell he was disgusted at the very idea of them working together.

'You know I'm right,' the little alien said.

'I know no such thing,' the HighBreed repiled.

Echo Echo shrugged. He didn't enjoy the idea of working with the HighBreed, but he'd enjoy being eaten by a Dravek even less. 'I don't like this any better than you do,' he said.

Looking past the HighBreed he spotted for the first time that there were two suns in the sky. No wonder the place was so hot.

'Um, how do we get off this, um, planet-whatever-it's-called?'

'We are on Turrawuste, a desert world,

useful only as a teleporter relay station,' the HighBreed told him.

'So how come we didn't beam in near the teleporter machine?'

'The damage to the pod must have temporarily shifted the focusing axis.'

'Can you fix it?'

The HighBreed growled. 'If we find the teleporter pod on this planet, we won't need to fix it,' he said. 'Simply avoid hitting it with a rock while it is activated.'

'OK, smart guy,' replied Echo Echo. 'Where is it?'

'Impossible to tell.'

'Impossible for you, maybe.' Echo Echo opened his mouth wider than ever before and let out a deafening sonic shriek. He listened to it roll off into the distance. Then, very faintly, he heard a soft ping as the sonar detected something metal.

'That way,' Echo Echo said, pointing in

the direction of the sound. 'It'll take a day or more to reach it on foot. Let's go.'

He began to walk, but quickly realised the HighBreed wasn't following.

'C'mon, alien dude, the sooner we get moving, the sooner we get home,' said Ben. 'Then we'll both be happy.'

'Your kind disgusts me,' seethed the HighBreed.

'Huh? What did you say?'

'I will not allow such a filthy creature to spend a single moment longer in my presence.'

'Creeps you out? Hey, I can take care of that. Watch this.'

With a flash, Echo Echo transformed back into Ben. 'See? I'm really just a plain ol' human.'

'That is even worse!' bellowed the HighBreed. 'Be gone, foul thing. I shall traverse to the teleporter alone.'

Suddenly, the roar of a Dravek boomed across the sand. It sounded far away, but close enough to be worrying.

'We have to watch each other's backs,' said Ben. 'We don't want any more Draveks to drop in on us. Or under us. If you know what I mean . . .'

Yet again, the HighBreed made no sign of moving. He turned his head sharply.

'Now what?' Ben sighed.

'If I am forced to travel with you, then you must keep ten paces behind me at all times.'

'But I'm the one who knows the way,' Ben reminded him.

'Ten paces!'

Ben shook his head and sighed. 'Fine. Whatever. Just get moving.'

Satisfied, the HighBreed started walking. Ben counted ten paces, shook his head again, then set off across the desert.

The planet's twin suns blazed down on them and scorched the sand beneath their feet as they slowly made their way towards the distant teleporter.

Wiping the sweat from his forehead, Ben joked, 'Phew! Hot enough for you?'

'Yes.'

'No, see, I wasn't really asking,' said Ben. 'It's just an expression. It means it's hot out.'

'It is obviously hot,' spat the HighBreed. 'I do not see the point of reiterating what we both already know.'

'Sheesh,' said Ben. 'Makes me glad I didn't say "it's not the heat, it's the humidity".'

'There is no humidity,' the big alien snapped. 'It is, in fact, the heat.'

'I know,' Ben mumbled. 'Just trying to make conversation.'

Then without warning, the HighBreed stumbled and fell forwards on to the sand. Ben rushed over to see what was wrong.

'Do not lay your hands on me, vile thing,' barked the HighBreed as Ben approached.

Ben hesitated, then quickly removed his jacket and held it out for the alien. 'Here, you can use this to keep the sun off your head. It'll help to protect you.'

The HighBreed knocked the jacket away. 'I do not take charity from vermin. I merely require a moment's rest.'

'Rest won't cut it, I'm afraid. You're dehydrated already.'

'The one true species thrives in a much

cooler climate.'

'Humans like it cooler than this, too. But
you're actually wasting away here. I've got
something that can help us both beat the heat.
Hang on.'

SLAM!

Ben smacked his hand against the face of
the Omnitrix. A familiar green glow wrapped
itself around him, changing him into another of
his alien forms.

'Big Chill!' he cried, unfurling his wide,
moth-like wings and springing up into the air.

'What are you doing, foul creature?' the
HighBreed hissed. 'Stay away from me.'

'Hey, I'm watching your back, dude,' Big
Chill replied, hovering over the HighBreed. 'It's
time to cool down!'

Taking a deep breath, Big Chill suddenly
blasted out a cloud of icy cold air across the
HighBreed's back.

'Desist,' said the HighBreed, weakly. 'Stop that this instant.'

Big Chill stopped blowing. 'Why?'

'I did not request your assistance.'

'I know. Chill, dude.' His mouth curved into a wide grin. 'Ha! See what I did there?'

'I do not.'

'I made a little pun,' smiled Big Chill. 'See, I . . . hey, what's that?' Big Chill's smile slowly faded as he stared off across the desert, to where a patch of blue liquid was shimmering in the sand. 'Water!'

'Your powers of deduction are truly staggering,' said the HighBreed, sarcastically.

'Uh, whatever. I'm going to get a drink,' announced Big Chill, fluttering off in the direction of the water pool. 'I'll bring some back for you.'

Landing softly beside the oasis, Big Chill reached out a hand. The "water" felt warm and slimy to the touch. He sniffed it, trying to work out what it was. The smell was familiar – he'd smelled it only recently.

Oh, no!

Big Chill suddenly remembered where he had smelled this stuff before. Inside the Dravek.

He spun around in time to see the jagged teeth of the worm-creature rise up from beneath the sand all around him. The liquid wasn't water, it was saliva. He'd flown straight into a Dravek's trap!

As the teeth closed in around him, Big Chill launched himself skyward. Using his alien abilities he passed through the teeth as if he were a ghost. He emerged on the other side, leaving a layer of thick ice over the worm-creature's mouth.

While the Dravek shook off the ice, Big Chill flew back to the HighBreed. 'It was a trap,' he told him.

Huge chunks of ice began to fall away from the Dravek's mouth.

'That thing's getting loose,' warned Big Chill. 'Come on – we've got to move.'

'You cannot issue commands to me, mongrel. Lesser beings do my bidding. You will do as I say.' The HighBreed stood up just as the Dravek shook off the last of the ice from its huge mouth. It began to squirm in their direction, showing its razor-sharp teeth. The HighBreed then turned to Big Chill. 'I bid you to fight.'

'Oh, all right then. If you say so!' said Big Chill, wrapping up in an invisible cloak.

Beating his wings, Big Chill raced over to the Dravek and phased through its body. At the alien's touch, a layer of ice began to spread across the worm-creature's skin.

KERAAACK!

Twisting its body, the Dravek shattered the ice into fragments. As the pieces hit the sand they began to melt almost at once. Big Chill launched another attack. This time, he hit the monster right in its eyes, but the Dravek shattered the ice immediately.

'It's not working!' Big Chill cried, as the Dravek shook off yet another ice blast.

Roaring in triumph, the Dravek pulled itself up to its full height, opened its mouth, and prepared to strike.

CHAPTER THREE

KILLER CREEPY CRAWLIES

'We can't keep this up much longer,' hissed Big Chill.

'Follow my lead,' barked the HighBreed.

'And do what?'

'Freeze him.'

'Already tried that.'

'From inside,' the HighBreed said. 'Stay inside. Keep him frozen until I say otherwise.'

Big Chill didn't much like the idea of hanging about in the Dravek's insides, but there was no time for argument. Flying upwards he disappeared inside the creature's mouth and raced down its throat.

The HighBreed watched as the worm-creature began to slow. Its red skin went a dark shade of blue, before crystals of white ice began to form on the surface. In just a few moments the entire worm was encased in a shell of thick white frost.

'Now!' the HighBreed bellowed, raising both hands high up into the air. As Big Chill phased, ghost-like, from within the beast, the HighBreed fired twenty or more pointed spikes up into the ice.

The frozen worm started to vibrate. Then it let out an ear-splitting roar. The ice shattered into a thousand little pieces and the Dravek retreated back underground.

The HighBreed sunk back down onto the baking hot desert floor. He was boiling hot. Big Chill knew he had to help the HighBreed cool down. Taking a deep breath, he got ready with another blast of cold air.

'Don't you dare,' the HighBreed seethed. 'Leave me be. Now that the danger has passed, I can locate water myself.'

A flap of skin on the alien's chest pulled back, making way for two long tendrils. The tendrils looked like the roots of a plant, but wriggled like snakes as they burrowed deep down into the sand.

'Ew,' Big Chill muttered. 'Gross.'

'There is water below the sand, if one looks deep enough,' the HighBreed said. Just then, liquid began to bubble up from where his tendrils had entered the ground. 'There.'

'I didn't know you HighBreeds were some kind of plant.'

'We are not "some kind" of anything. The HighBreed is the only kind.'

And with that, he began to drink.

A few minutes later, Ben was finishing the last of the water. It tasted better than anything he had ever drunk before, and he could already feel some of his strength returning.

The HighBreed, too, looked much stronger. He was up on his feet, resuming the march towards the teleporter. Ben was about to follow when he heard a faint scratching sound.

'Did you hear something?' Ben asked, glancing at the ground around them.

Ten paces in front, the HighBreed didn't bother looking back. 'I heard nothing. Except you, human. Which is the same as nothing.'

'Ha. Ha,' Ben said, not laughing.

'I believe I am beginning to grasp your concept of "humour".' He was about to continue when the ground beneath him trembled. The HighBreed stopped, his muscles tensed.

'Uh, oh. More Draveks underground?' whispered Ben.

The HighBreed shook his head. 'Worse.'

'C'mon,' gulped Ben. 'Worse?'

From behind them the scratching sound came again. Ben whipped around and gasped at what he saw. An area of desert about the size of a football pitch was moving as if it were alive. As Ben and the HighBreed watched, thousands of armoured creepy crawlies scurried from beneath the sand.

'Dasypodidae,' said the HighBreed, recognising the creatures.

'They're little,' smiled Ben. 'How could these guys possibly be worse than Draveks?'

The answer came right away. Dozens of the little bugs clambered up Ben's legs and over

his body, almost covering him completely. He
thrashed around, trying to shake them away.

'Get them off me!'

The HighBreed was in no position to help.
Hundreds of the Dasypodidae were scurrying all
over him, dragging him to the ground. He and
Ben both fell at the same time, and were quickly
covered by a living carpet of the killer insects.

A burst of bright green light briefly
illuminated the heaving mass, as Ben
transformed into Swampfire.

'This'll only take a second,' he said, hurling huge fireballs down towards the bugs. His eyes flicked up and he realised there were several thousand more rushing in to replace the ones he had burned. 'Did I say a second? I'm now thinking more like an hour.'

Glancing around, Swampfire spotted an area of rocky ground. 'HighBreed, this way,' he called, racing up the hill towards the rocks.

Summoning all his strength, the HighBreed dragged himself in the direction of Swampfire's voice, kicking off the insects as he scrambled up the hillside.

When the HighBreed was out of harm's way, Swampfire blasted a mound of rocks with a ball of flame. The stone crumbled and began to roll down the hill, causing a landslide. The tumbling boulders forced the insects back, and soon they were buried beneath a flowing river of sand.

As the ground gave way beneath his feet,

the HighBreed began to fall. He slid down the hillside, his arms flailing wildly as he tried to slow himself down.

A powerful hand reached down and caught him by the arm. With a grunt, Swampfire hoisted the HighBreed back up onto the rock beside him.

'You're welcome,' smirked Swampfire, when it was obvious the alien wasn't about to thank him.

'How dare . . . You filthy . . .' The HighBreed yanked his arm away. 'Unhand me!'

'What is with you?' demanded Swampfire. 'Yeah, you don't like the creatures I turn into, I get it. But c'mon, I was saving you. Cut an alien monster guy some slack once in a while.'

Angrily, Swampfire turned and stomped off across the desert. The HighBreed sat on the rock, not moving, until Swampfire returned.

With a dramatic sigh, Swampfire held out his hands, gesturing for the HighBreed to take the lead. The HighBreed alien stood up and began to walk, leaving Swampfire behind to follow in his footsteps.

'"Ten paces behind",' Swampfire mumbled, before setting off after the HighBreed.

Several hours later, as the twin suns were beginning to dip below the horizon, Swampfire was still muttering below his breath. 'The second we're off this planet I'll show him "ten paces behind",' he seethed.

Up ahead, the cool night air was giving the HighBreed new strength. He strode on, paying no attention to his companion.

'This is as good a place as any to set up camp for the night,' Swampfire announced, stopping by a rocky outcrop.

'No. We shall walk through the night.'

'No,' insisted Swampfire, mimicking the HighBreed's serious tone. 'We shall camp here for the night.'

'I would not use such an insolent tone with me, lesser creature,' growled the HighBreed, spinning to face him.

'Oh, really?'

'You have not yet dealt with me at my full strength. See how the cool night air has begun to restore me?'

Swampfire nodded. 'Yeah. I noticed.'

'I shall carry on from here on my own.'

'All right, go then,' replied Swampfire.

'You have outstayed your usefulness to me,' continued the HighBreed, resuming his march across the sand.

'So have you!'

The HighBreed hadn't got very far when a piercing cry of a Dravek echoed around the desert planet. The HighBreed stopped in his tracks. He looked back at Swampfire, then off into the still darkness that lay ahead. At last he reached a decision.

'We shall camp here for the night,' he said, as if it had been his idea in the first place, and then he hurried back to join Swampfire by the rocks.

'Sure thing. Whatever you say, tough guy,' Swampfire replied.

CHAPTER FOUR

WOUNDED

Night had fallen on the desert. The flickering flames of a small campfire were the only defence against the darkness. Ben sat by the flames, enjoying the heat they gave off. The desert could get very cold at night.

'Pull up a boulder,' Ben suggested, turning to the HighBreed. 'Sit down.'

'So your infernal pit can deplete me of my strength? I think not.'

'It's a campfire. It's tradition,' explained Ben, patiently. 'You sit around it and, you know, maybe sing a song. Eat a hotdog. Talk.'

'Talk? To you?' snorted the HighBreed. 'For what conceivable purpose?'

Ben felt a little of his patience drain away, but he continued. 'My name is Ben, Ben Tennyson. What's your name?'

'I am called Reinrassig the Third, seventh son of the noble HighBreed house of Di Razza, direct descendent of the pure-blooded High Order of Rasecht, heir to the –'

'I'm gonna call you "Reiny",' said Ben, cutting him off.

'That is very disrespectful, Ben-Ben Tennyson.'

Ben shrugged and poked at the fire with a stick. The flames flared brighter. 'It's weird. Despite the fact that I honestly don't trust you any farther than Humungousaur could throw you, it's still pretty cool how we've managed to work together to survive.' He dropped the stick and warmed his hands on the fire's glow.

'I mean, we may not be the best of friends exactly, but we're not full-on mortal enemies any more either.'

'You and I will always be enemies,' the HighBreed replied.

'But we've been able to see past our differences. Probably because I know what it's like to be . . . well, not a HighBreed exactly, but a whole bunch of other kinds of alien creatures kinda like you.' He held up his wrist so the HighBreed could see the Omnitrix. 'Thanks to this, I get to walk a mile in other life forms' shoes. So I can totally understand what it's like to be them, since I have been them.'

Ben sat back and nodded, proud of his little speech. For a moment the HighBreed said nothing, staring off into the distance. Then he began to speak. 'Such presumption,' he growled. 'But what else is to be expected from a genetically inferior creature?'

'I don't . . . what?'

'Why would I, a HighBreed, be the slightest bit interested in befriending the revolting likes of you?'

'I'm just trying to be nice here,' Ben protested. 'Find some common ground or something.'

'You and I are more than mere enemies,' said the HighBreed, drawing himself up to his full impressive height. 'HighBreeds were the very first race in the universe. All species hence, other than pure-blooded HighBreeds, are nothing but mongrels. Hideous abominations of nature, especially humans.

'As soon as I no longer require your aid for my own protection, Ben-Ben Tennyson, I shall eradicate you. And there will be one less vermin infesting a grateful universe.'

'You can't really believe all that,' replied Ben. 'Not after everything we've been through. Not after the way I've been helping you.'

'When you weren't trying to kill me.'

Ben was too angry and frustrated to come up with a reply. Instead he shook his head and stared into the heart of the fire.

'You are tired, human,' said the HighBreed. 'I shall take the first watch.'

Ben's eyes narrowed suspiciously. Like he'd said, he didn't trust the HighBreed one bit.

'Oh, no,' Ben said, 'I'm wide awake. You get some sleep. I'll take the first watch.'

Neither of them had given in, but in the end it was Ben who finally fell asleep first. He lay flat on his back, snoring below his breath.

A shadow passed over him, but Ben

didn't stir. The HighBreed stared down at him, his alien eyes narrowed in disgust. Then, with a sudden jerk of his shoulder, the HighBreed raised an arm above his head.

Sensing danger, Ben flicked open his eyes. He let out a sharp gasp as he spotted the HighBreed's huge fist swinging swiftly down towards him.

SPLAAAAK!

The HighBreed's claws snapped shut

around a large bug. It looked like the ones they had fought earlier, only this one was much larger and more deadly looking. It squirmed in the alien's grip, twisting its body until its powerful jaws were free.

The bug's mouth snapped tightly shut around the HighBreed's wrist, causing the alien to cry out in agony. The insect then forced its jaws closed further. The HighBreed howled as his hand dropped onto the sand with a plop. Pausing only to hiss at Ben, the alien bug scuttled off across the sand.

'Can you regenerate it?' asked Ben, his eyes locked on the HighBreed's severed hand.

'I am not a lowly Homo Palustris,' the HighBreed snapped, referring to the alien race from which Swampfire came.

'But it can be healed?'

'Not from such an injury as this. Not in these conditions,' replied the HighBreed, writhing in pain.

Ben's mind raced. There had to be some way to heal the HighBreed's arm. But how?

And then it hit him. Homo Palustris.

Swampfire!

Ben quickly slammed down on the Omnitrix. In a flash of green light, Ben transformed into the flame-headed plant alien. He collected the HighBreed's hand from the sand. Kneeling in front of the injured alien, Swampfire carefully pressed the hand against the stump of the wrist. Four or five tiny green pods fell from his own hand and began to burrow into the wound.

In moments the pods began to grow. As the HighBreed watched on, thin strands of plant vine wrapped tightly around the injury, reconnecting his hand to his arm.

The HighBreed held his arm up in the air. He twitched the fingers. It hurt, but at least it worked.

Swampfire changed back into Ben. 'Better?' he asked.

'Why would you help me?' the HighBreed demanded. 'It was in my own interest to stop that creature from harming you.'

'Yeah?' said Ben. 'Well, it's in my interest to help anybody who needs it.'

The HighBreed turned away, Ben's words still ringing in his ears. Maybe, just maybe, there was a little bit more to the human race than he thought.

Ben perched on a rock and poked his stick into the fire again. The flames were dying down. He would have to go and find more sticks to burn soon.

A sudden rumble beneath him made Ben leap up to his feet. The rock he had been sitting on trembled and shook. The HighBreed extended an arm and fired a dozen razor-sharp spikes at the stone. Almost at once, the rumbling stopped.

Ben flashed the HighBreed a grateful smile and crept back over to where he had been sitting. Cautiously, he prodded the stone with his foot. Nothing happened. Whatever had been making the rock move had now –

KRAKA-BOOOOM!

Sand suddenly erupted all around him like a huge volcanic explosion, sending rocks, stones and boulders rocketing up towards the night sky.

Ben was thrown right off balance. The wind was knocked from him as he fell and rolled backwards across the ground.

The sand and dust were carried quickly away on the breeze, revealing Ben's worst nightmare. A Dravek reared up from the sand, its wide jaws snapping and snarling. But this wasn't just any Dravek, it was the biggest Dravek they had seen so far.

And it was bearing directly down on top of Ben.

CHAPTER FIVE

CHANGES

A volley of sharp spikes embedded themselves deep in the Dravek's tough hide, distracting the creature and drawing it away from Ben. The giant worm twisted its bulky body and lunged towards the HighBreed, who had just enough time to fire off a few more shots before leaping out of the way.

The cool night air was boosting the HighBreed's strength, but his arm was still healing and he wasn't yet at full fighting fitness. As the worm-creature turned once again and raced towards him, the HighBreed had no choice but to flee for his life.

'Ben-Ben Tennyson!' he bellowed, feeling the ground beneath him quake. Still dazed from his fall, Ben looked up to see the HighBreed darting towards him, with the

Dravek right behind.

Ben was too groggy to move yet. There was no way he could get clear in time. Realising this, the HighBreed stopped, turned, then threw himself towards the Dravek's open mouth. Gripping onto the creature's jagged lips he hung there, not quite sure what to do next.

Luckily Ben was back in action. He scrambled upright and snatched a burning stick from the campfire. There was no time to go hero – he had to act and he had to act fast.

Racing back to the Dravek's mouth, Ben hurled the flaming piece of wood down its throat. The mouth snapped shut immediately, throwing the HighBreed down on to the hard-packed sand.

Thick plumes of grey smoke billowed from within the Dravek, as its toxic stomach acids caught light. It wriggled and squirmed, thrashing its powerful tail against the sand.

At last the creature opened its jaws. A jet of flame emerged, like the breath of some alien dragon, and the fire inside the Dravek went out. Ben and the HighBreed braced themselves for the battle to resume, but the worm-creature had taken enough punishment for one night. With a final snarl it burrowed its tail into the ground and sunk down out of sight.

Taking a deep breath to calm his racing heart, Ben turned to the alien at his side.

'Maybe you were right,' he admitted. 'Maybe we should walk all night.'

And walk they did. For hours they trudged across the darkened desert, watching each other's backs as they made their way towards the teleporter. Although Ben didn't say it, he was glad to have the HighBreed with him. He would never have survived on his own.

'Thanks for saving me back there,' he said. 'Again.'

The HighBreed didn't respond, choosing instead to carry on walking in silence.

'This is a huge thing,' continued Ben, excitedly. 'A sign of personal growth. Proof that underneath it all, HighBreeds aren't really so bad. That despite those terrible things you may have said before, you really do want to try to be friends with a human.'

Ben upped his pace, walking now with a spring in his step. Even though he was millions of miles from home on a desolate alien planet, he felt good. He was helping to change the HighBreed, and change him for the better.

But once again the HighBreed did not answer. He kept walking, one foot plodding steadily in front of the other, lost in his own troubling thoughts. The human was walking alongside him, not behind him.

And for some reason he couldn't understand, the HighBreed didn't mind.

It was morning when they finally reached the teleporter pod. It stood before them, scuffed by sand and bleached by the sun, but otherwise exactly like the one that had carried them to this desert world.

'There it is, come on!' yelped Ben, racing across the sand towards the machine. He stopped just a few paces on, when he realised the HighBreed wasn't following. 'Not the ten paces behind thing again?'

The HighBreed looked down, then slowly raised his head again. 'Go home, Ben-Ben Tennyson,' he said. 'I shall remain here.'

'Did you hit your head or something?' asked Ben, unable to believe what he was hearing. 'There's the teleporter. We can finally get off this sand trap of doom and back to our own lives.'

'I have spent too long with you, Ben-Ben Tennyson,' the alien said, and Ben couldn't miss the sadness in his voice. 'And have therefore myself become contaminated.'

Ben raised an eyebrow. 'Contaminated?'

'As clearly evidenced by my uncharacteristic behaviour, risking my own life to save you, a lowly human,' said the HighBreed.

'Reiny,' began Ben, softly, 'what you did was a good thing.'

'I have obviously become infected by your mongrel influence and am now unclean.'

Ben rounded on him. 'Listen, big guy, even if I believed that was true, why would you stay here?'

'In self-imposed exile. As it should be.' The HighBreed craned his neck and looked up at the two burning suns raging in the sky. 'For I can never, ever return back home. Or anywhere in fact. I could be in danger of infecting the rest of my kind. The only honourable choice is for me to remain here forever.'

'No,' said Ben.

'Because all lesser beings other than pure, unadulterated HighBreeds must be expunged from the universe.' The alien paused before adding, 'Including myself.'

'I thought I had gotten through to you,' said Ben. 'I thought you had changed.'

'This much is true. I have changed,' agreed the HighBreed. 'And now I must pay the price. I must accept this punishment. It is the only way. Goodbye Ben-Ben Tennyson.'

    A thousand light years away, in a
warehouse on the other side of the universe,
Kevin and Gwen were poking around in the
control panel of the teleporter. Everything
seemed to be connected properly – the wires
were in place, the switches were correctly
aligned – but the thing refused to do anything.
It was completely dead.

'Everything looks fine,' Kevin said, for the hundredth time in the last few hours. 'But I can't make it work.'

Gwen leaned over his shoulder, studying the machine. She was tired – they both were – but they couldn't give up.

'We've got to fix it, Kevin,' she urged. 'We have to find –'

Suddenly, a flickering blue light shimmered across the surface of the teleporter. Kevin and Gwen stepped away just as a very familiar figure stumbled through.

'Ben! You're back!' cried Gwen, rushing to meet her cousin. She threw her arms around him and they shared a warm hug.

Even Kevin looked happy to see his friend. 'Man, am I glad to see you. You gave us a big scare,' he smiled, punching Ben playfully on the arm. 'We've been trying to fix that thing for hours. We thought we'd lost you big time! Where did you go?'

'It's a long story. Just think giant sand

monsters, deadly flesh-eating bugs and a whole lot of heat.'

'Hang on, where did the HighBreed go?' Gwen asked. 'Did he get away?'

Ben looked to the floor and shook his head, sadly. 'No, I doubt it.'

Back on the deadly desert world of Turrawuste, the HighBreed sat high up on a rock examining his arm. Swampfire's vines were doing their job, and the wound was knitting together nicely. The hand had taken on a strange green tinge – the only outward sign of how his encounter with Ben-Ben Tennyson had contaminated him.

But it was the contamination inside that really mattered. The HighBreed knew it was wrong, he knew he must be sick, or mad, or both, but despite their differences he had actually found himself almost liking the strange human boy. He had felt a strange connection with the enemy.

With a shudder he stood up and stretched his tired limbs. He was hot and thirsty. He didn't have the energy to look for water in the ground. The twin suns shone brightly in the morning sky, scorching his skin and draining all of his strength. Perhaps, he decided, that was for the best.

Clambering up to the top of a rocky hill, the HighBreed took up a position atop the highest boulder. Standing up straight he stared off into the distance where he could see three huge Draveks thundering across the sand. They were too far away for him to feel the shaking of the ground, but it would not be long, he knew, until he felt the first tremors.

He looked up to the sky and nodded, satisfied that he had chosen the correct fate.

He was contaminated. Filthy. Impure. And impurity had to be destroyed. All of it.

Even him.